BALLPARK
Mysteries 5
THE
ALL-STAR
JOKER

BALLPARK Mysteries 5
THE ALL-STAR JOKER

by David A. Kelly
illustrated by Mark Meyers

A STEPPING STONE BOOK™

Random House 🏠 New York

This book is dedicated to my two favorite all-stars, Steven and Scott.
—D.A.K.

To Dominic, Amy, Zach, and Josh —M.M.

"There is no homework."
—Dan Quisenberry, Kansas City Royals pitcher,
on the best thing about baseball

Text copyright © 2012 by David A. Kelly
Cover art and interior illustrations copyright © 2012 by Mark Meyers

All rights reserved.
Published in the United States by Random House Children's Books, a division of Random House, Inc., New York.

Random House and the colophon are registered trademarks and A Stepping Stone Book and the colophon are trademarks of Random House, Inc.

Visit us on the Web!
SteppingStonesBooks.com
randomhouse.com/kids

Educators and librarians, for a variety of teaching tools, visit us at randomhouse.com/teachers

Library of Congress Cataloging-in-Publication Data
Kelly, David A. (David Andrew)
The All-Star joker / by David A. Kelly ; illustrated by Mark Meyers. — 1st ed.
p.   cm. — (Ballpark mysteries ; 5)
Summary: When cousins Mike and Kate go to Kansas City for the All-Star game, they meet the son of the American League starting catcher who stands falsely accused of playing practical jokes on his All-Star teammates.
ISBN 978-0-375-86884-9 (pbk.) — ISBN 978-0-375-96884-6 (lib. bdg.) — ISBN 978-0-375-89967-6 (ebook)
[1. All-Star Baseball Game—Fiction. 2. Baseball—Fiction. 3. Practical jokes—Fiction. 4. Mystery and detective stories.] I. Meyers, Mark, ill. II. Title.
PZ7.K2936Al 2012 [Fic]—dc23 2011034706

Printed in the United States of America

10 9 8 7 6 5 4 3 2 1

Contents

A Last-Minute Scratch

The crowd roared as the Kansas City Royals catcher Josh Robinson belted another ball high into the warm July night.

"I got it! I got it!" Kate Hopkins yelled. She ran backward across the outfield grass. Her cousin Mike Walsh and a gangly kid with dark curly hair started for the ball, too, but Kate waved them off.

PLOP! The baseball dropped perfectly into her glove. She showed it to Mike. Stamped on it in big blue letters were the words HOME RUN DERBY.

"Nice catch, cuz! Our first home run derby ball!" Mike said, pounding his fist into his glove. "If only we could stay out here to field balls during the all-star game!"

Kate and Mike were at the Kansas City Royals Kauffman Stadium for the all-star game. The all-star game was played each July in a different city. The best players from the American League took on the best players from the National League. The night before the all-star game was the home run derby.

The two cousins had flown in the day before from Cooperstown, New York, with Kate's mother. Mrs. Hopkins was a reporter for the American Sportz website. Last summer Mike and Kate had volunteered in a special program that helped kids with disabilities play baseball. Some of the volunteers had been invited to chase balls in the outfield during the home run derby.

"I can't believe I caught a ball hit by Josh Robinson!" Kate said. "He's one of the best catchers in the league!"

"You bet he is," said the gangly boy who had been chasing the ball Kate caught. His bright blue T-shirt had ROYALS written in white script across the front. "He's my dad!"

The boy turned and pointed over his shoulders to the big white letters that arched across his back. They spelled ROBINSON. Underneath was 23.

"Your dad's Josh Robinson?" Kate asked. "Really?"

The boy turned back around. "Yup," he said with a smile. "My name is Andy."

"I'm Kate. And this is my cousin Mike," she

said. "You should probably have this, then."
She flipped the home run derby baseball to
Andy.

Andy shook his head. He tossed the ball
back to Kate. "Nah, you keep it," he said.
"We've got plenty of baseballs at home. But

this is the first time Dad's been in the home run derby. What are you guys doing here?"

"We volunteered last summer in the Little League Challenger Division," Mike said. "They invited us to the all-star game."

Andy tipped his hat to Kate and Mike. "Cool," he said. "My dad volunteers, too. He does magic tricks and tells baseball jokes when he visits kids in the hospital. They love it. You just have to watch it when he starts with the practical jokes! He likes playing tricks on people."

CRACK! The sound of another hit echoed through the outfield.

"Heads-up!" Kate yelled. "Your dad nailed that one!"

The kids in the outfield ran back toward the right-field wall. But the ball sailed over their heads. It flew past a row of seats toward the longest fountain Mike had ever seen. It was just behind the outfield wall. A second black fountain curved along the outfield on the left side.

SPLASH! The ball landed in the right-field fountain. Jets of water surged fifteen feet up in the air, while red, yellow, and blue lights shone up from under the water.

"I guess your dad really went deep on that one," Mike said. He elbowed Kate in the ribs. "Get it?"

Kate rolled her eyes at Mike's joke. "Funny," she said. "But not funny enough to *gush* over!"

Up at home plate, Josh waited for the next pitch. He was the sixth of eight batters in the home run derby. But he had the lowest score and only one out left. Unless he hit a lot of home runs, his turn would be done.

The next pitch was right over the plate. Josh

popped the ball high to left field for an out.

"Shoot!" Andy said. "Only three home runs. That's not enough to advance."

"Sorry," Mike said. "Want to stay out here with us? Big D is up next. We're friends with him. We helped him find his lucky bat when it was stolen."

"Cool!" Andy said. "Sure, I'll stay."

Big D from the Boston Red Sox strode to the plate. The stadium full of fans went wild. With his friendly smile and home run record, Big D was a favorite to win the derby. He stepped into the batter's box. He swiveled his front foot in the dirt and took a few practice swings.

Mike, Kate, and Andy got ready. Part of Mike wanted Big D to nail home runs over the fence to win. But another part wanted him to hit some pop-ups for them to catch.

Big D let the first two pitches go by. But

he unwound on the third pitch and sent it sailing to the left of the huge center-field scoreboard topped by a giant gold crown. The fans cheered wildly!

Kate, though, was watching Big D, not the ball. "What's wrong with Big D? He's dancing around like he's got ants in his pants!"

She was right. Big D hopped around home plate as if his feet were on fire. He twitched his shoulders from one side to the other. Then he reached his bat over his shoulder and rubbed it up and down his back quickly as if he had an itch he couldn't scratch. After a minute, he settled down and tried to hit again.

But something still bothered him. As the pitch flew over the plate, Big D's shoulder twisted in a funny way and the bat weakly hit the ball down the first-base line. It was not his night.

Big D looked like a big dud. Pitch after pitch went by. In between them, Big D kept scratching his stomach and his back and rubbing his feet. Whenever he hit a ball, it dribbled into the outfield.

Big D's turn ended quickly. He only scored one home run, the lowest score all night.

Kate winced. "That was awful! Big D should have hit a lot of home runs!"

Mike nudged Andy with his elbow. "Well, at least your father's not in last place anymore," he said.

Andy cracked a smile. "Hey, you're right!" he said.

"Come on. Let's go see what happened," Kate said.

While the final batter stepped up to the plate, Mike, Kate, and Andy ran to the American League's dugout. Andy jogged over to his dad, who was standing next to Sparky, the team's manager.

"What's going on?" Andy asked.

Josh shrugged. "I don't know," he said. "Maybe Big D's allergic to all that prairie grass we have around here."

Big D stood at the top of the dugout steps, scratching his arms like crazy. "Ah, looks like he's just allergic to hitting home runs on his night off," muttered Sparky. "I say you either get the job done or you don't. Big D didn't tonight. I sure hope he does better during the game tomorrow."

Still, Big D smiled when he spotted Mike and Kate.

"Mike and Kate! Good to see you," Big D wheezed, in between scratches. "I don't need help finding my bat tonight. But I'd love if you could figure out why I'm so itchy."

"Maybe it's your uniform," Mike said. "Once I was allergic to laundry detergent. It left a bunch of red marks on my arm."

"Nah, we brought the uniforms with us," Big D panted. "Arrrrgh! This is killing me! Mike, can you grab my water bottle from my locker?"

"Sure," Mike replied. He scampered down the steps into the clubhouse behind the dugout. While he was gone, Big D leaned into the edge of the dugout and rubbed his back against it. Then he whipped off his hat and used both hands to scratch his head. Finally, Mike returned with the water bottle. Big D took three huge gulps and gasped for air.

"I'm still itchy, but that feels better," he said, wiping his chin. "Thanks!" He went back to scratching furiously.

Mike made a funny face at Kate. It looked

as if he had something important to say.

"Uh, Big D?" he said. "I found something in the locker room that you might want to see."

Big D stopped scratching his legs. He looked at Mike.

Mike pulled out a small plastic bottle from his back pocket. He held it up.

Across the front, it read:

ITCHING POWDER

Rocketing
to the Top

Before Big D could respond, Sparky grabbed the bottle from Mike's hand.

"Itching powder!" Sparky read the words aloud. He flipped the bottle open and tipped it upside down. "Empty. Well, I'll be . . ."

Sparky squinted down at Mike. Wisps of white wiry hair poked out from under the edge of his baseball cap. "Where'd you get this, son?"

"I found it in the trash can in the locker

room," Mike said. "Right next to the door."

"Hmph," Sparky snorted. He snapped around and stamped to the edge of the dugout where Josh stood. Sparky fixed his eyes on Josh. He held up the empty bottle.

"Robinson, I was warned about your practical jokes," Sparky said. "Don't pull any more. Have all the fun you want with your regular team. I'm here to win the all-star game for the American League, and I'm going to do it with you or without you."

Josh took a step back. "Whoa! Coach, I—I didn't have anything to do with that!" he sputtered. "Everyone knows that I like practical jokes. But I don't know anything about that itching powder."

Sparky scowled and pointed a finger at Josh. "I won't tolerate any jokes on my team," he said. He slipped the bottle into his pocket

and tramped down the stairs into the clubhouse. Still scratching his hip, Big D headed for the showers to wash off the itching powder.

Andy pounded his fist into the palm of his other hand. "That's not fair," he said to Mike and Kate. "My dad didn't do it!"

"Nice job getting on the good side of our manager, Josh," said one of the other players.

"That's Robert 'Rocket' Richards, from the Toronto Blue Jays," Andy whispered to Kate and Mike. "He and my dad are the two catchers for the American League team. But the Rocket *is* a better hitter."

"Hey, Josh. Since you're such an expert on itching powder, what do sheep use to scratch an itch?" the Rocket taunted Andy's dad.

Josh grimaced and shook his head. "I don't know, Rocket. What?"

The Rocket smiled. "A *lamb* post!" he said. "Get it? Instead of a lamppost. A lamb post!"

Josh rolled his eyes. "Oh brother! I don't need this," he said. "I'm going to check my equipment." He headed down the stairs to the clubhouse.

"Aww, you're just sore because you only

hit three home runs in round one, and I hit eleven!" the Rocket gloated. "Looks like I'll be moving on to the finals and you won't!"

Just then, a man with a jutting chin, slicked-back black hair, and a fancy white suit brushed by Mike. He strode up to the Rocket and whispered something in his ear.

Kate tugged Mike's sleeve. She headed down the baseline. "Hey, guys, they're starting the final round," Kate said. "It's the Rocket versus Troy Young from the Colorado Rockies." She plopped down on the grass near third base. Andy and Mike sat down, too, stretching out their legs and resting back on their hands.

Troy Young went first. Mike, Kate, and Andy watched as he hit five more home runs. Young's total for the three rounds was twenty-six. That meant the Rocket needed six home runs to win.

As he walked back to the dugout, Young took off his hat and waved to the cheering fans. At the same time, the Rocket approached the plate. He stared out at the fountains in left field. He took a few practice swings and waited for the pitcher. The Rocket was all business.

Kate plucked a short piece of grass and stuck it in her mouth. "I don't know," she said. "There's something about him that I don't like."

The Rocket's first four hits were pop-ups. Then pitch after pitch, he waited patiently. Finally, he unloaded and hit four home runs in a row! The crowd went wild! He let two more pitches fly by and homered the next two.

The Rocket had won the home run derby! And he still had six more outs to go! A chant of "Rock-et, Rock-et, Rock-et" started. He smiled for a moment, waved his right hand for quiet, and turned back to the plate. The Rocket finished after five more home runs. He ended up with a total of thirty-two home runs for the night.

The Rocket swaggered off the field. Cameras clicked as he took a big swig of Power-Punch. He grabbed a towel and mopped his face. A few minutes later, an official presented him with a big silver trophy of two bats.

The official led the Rocket to the press conference for all the home run derby hitters. Two long tables had been set up along the first-base line. Reporters stood nearby, waiting to ask players questions.

Josh took a seat near the end. A player from the Milwaukee Brewers pulled out the chair next to him and sat down.

CRACK!

The chair splintered into pieces, and the

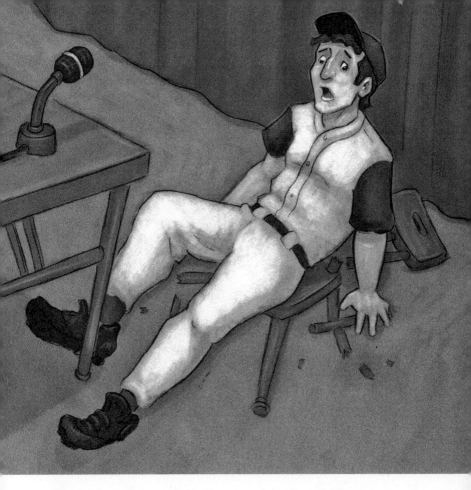

Brewers player fell flat on his butt! Everyone roared with laughter. As he stood up and dusted himself off, two stadium workers quickly piled the pieces of the broken chair against the infield wall and brought over a replacement.

"Oh, I guess Josh must have helped set up these chairs!" the Rocket said loud enough for everyone to hear.

From under his hat, Sparky glared at Andy's dad.

Josh tried to avoid Sparky's eyes. He looked at Andy, Kate, and Mike and shook his head.

"Or maybe it was too much of that great Kansas City barbecue," said Big D from the far end of the tables. "I know I had a lot of it last night! Now does anyone have questions for us?"

The reporters dove in with their questions.

Mike turned to Kate. She was frowning. "Are you thinking what I'm thinking?" he asked.

"Yes," Kate said. "Something's fishy here. I want to check out that chair."

Mike, Kate, and Andy sneaked over to the

infield wall. They poked through the remains of the chair. Andy picked up a leg.

"Guys! Look at this," he whispered. He pointed to the end of the leg. "It's a smooth cut here, and then there's a big, jagged break!"

"Someone used a saw to slice through it!" Mike said. "But they didn't cut it completely. That way the chair would break when someone sat in it. It was sabotage!"

Andy threw the chair leg to the ground. "There's no way that my father did this," he said. "He likes to pull pranks on people. But he wouldn't do it at the home run derby or the all-star game. Someone's trying to frame my dad!"

The Tables
Have Ears

The next morning, Mike and Kate pulled open the doors to the hotel restaurant at eight o'clock.

Mike rolled a baseball from hand to hand. "You really think this will work?" he asked.

Kate nodded. "Yup. As long as we don't get caught. How else are we going to find out what's going on?"

Mike and Kate were staying at the same hotel in Kansas City as the all-star players.

The night before with Andy, they had come up with a plan to spy on the players during breakfast.

They headed straight for a long breakfast buffet in the middle of the room.

With a wink, Kate picked up a napkin from the buffet table. She and Mike paused to examine the breakfast items. Mike looked longingly at the strips of crispy bacon and the steaming piles of blueberry pancakes. Kate leaned over the rows of strawberry and cinnamon muffins as if she were trying to decide on one.

"Ready?" she whispered. She glanced around the restaurant. The other people who had come in were busy finding tables.

"Ready," Mike said.

"Duck and cover!" Kate said. She dropped her napkin on the floor. Mike leaned down to tie his shoe. In seconds, they had lifted the

white cloth draped over the edge of the table and slid underneath.

Mike crossed his legs. "Now what?" he whispered. It was dark under the table.

"We wait and listen," Kate said. "If someone is trying to frame Andy's dad, he's probably from the National League team. Maybe he'll give away the plan!"

Kate positioned herself at the end of the table by the front of the restaurant. Mike hid about fifteen feet away, at the other end of the table.

Soon, people started coming through the buffet line. As they passed by, Mike and Kate could hear their conversations. It was easy to tell which people were baseball players. They were talking about teams, pitchers, or ballparks.

Nothing seemed out of the ordinary until Kate heard a raspy voice talking about the American League team. "Psst," she hissed softly to Mike. Kate cupped her ear with her hand to signal to listen closely.

"I'm just *itching* to see them bat," the man rasped. He snorted a little. "Especially after yesterday. It would be nice to see the American League lose for once."

Another man's voice responded with a chuckle. "Well, I'd like to see their winning streak fall apart like that chair!"

Kate slid over as the men moved down the buffet line. "They know about the itching powder and the broken chair!" she whispered. "Maybe they had something to do with it."

But before the men spoke again, something rustled at the edge of the table. A hand lifted the white drape. Their hiding place flooded with light. A waiter glared down at them.

Mike gulped. He tried to pretend he was looking for something. Kate simply stared back at the man.

"Can I help you?" the waiter asked. "If you'd like some food, you'll need to get in line like everyone else."

Kate shrugged. "We were just playing hide-and-seek," she said. "But we're finished. We're going to have breakfast."

"That's probably a good idea," the man said. He held the cloth up as Mike and Kate crawled out from under the table. As Kate did, she glanced at the men they had just over-heard. One was tall and skinny. The other was short with a bushy head of hair.

"Kate! Mike! I'm back here," Kate's mother called from a table in the corner. They rushed over to her, happy to leave the waiter behind. "I knew you two came down early, but I didn't see you here," Mrs. Hopkins said. "Where were you?"

"Oh, just playing a little hide-and-seek," Kate said. "But we're hungry now."

"I'll bet you are," Mrs. Hopkins said. "Perhaps that nice man in the white shirt can help you pick out some food."

Kate blushed. Mike fidgeted with his baseball.

"Anyway, take a look over there," Mrs. Hopkins said. "That's Home Run Harry. He held the record for home runs when I was a girl."

Mike straightened up to look. He tossed his baseball from his left hand to his right. "Think he'd autograph my ball?"

"Why don't you wait until he's done with breakfast and ask?" Mrs. Hopkins said. "For now, let's eat."

Mike, Kate, and Mrs. Hopkins heaped their

plates full of fruit, muffins, and pancakes. While they were eating, Mike and Kate kept an eye on the men they had overheard earlier.

"Hey, Mom," Kate said. "Do you know who those two men are? We heard them talking about the home run derby earlier."

Mrs. Hopkins studied the men for a moment. "Yes, the tall man is a trainer for the National League team. The short man is writing a book about one of the players."

"We were thinking they might have put the itching powder in Big D's uniform yesterday," Kate said. "They seemed to be laughing about it today."

"Well, it was pretty funny," Kate's mom said. "Unless you're Big D, of course. But I'm pretty sure they didn't do it. They would get in a lot of trouble if they did. Either of you want more juice?"

Kate and Mike shook their heads. While Mrs. Hopkins went to refill her glass, Kate and Mike scanned the room to see who else was there. Mike spotted Sparky and the manager for the National League team at one of the tables. Kate pointed out a group of pitchers at another table. The Rocket sat at a table near the front door. He was talking to the man in the fancy suit he had talked with yesterday.

When they finished breakfast, Mike glanced over at Home Run Harry. He was finishing a cup of coffee.

"Hang on just a minute," Mike said. He walked over to Harry and asked for an autograph. Kate watched as Harry signed the ball.

A minute later, Mike returned to the table, beaming from ear to ear. "He signed my baseball!" he said. Mike showed the ball to Kate's mom. Harry's signature was scrawled across the baseball's sweet spot.

"That's great!" Mrs. Hopkins said. She looked at her watch. "We should head out. I need to get to the ballpark early today."

Kate and Mike followed her. Mike was so busy looking at Home Run Harry's signature that he didn't notice a chair sticking out into the aisle near the front door.

"Oof!" Mike's left sneaker caught on the chair leg. He grabbed the back of the chair to steady himself, but the ball popped out of his hand. It bounced and rolled along the carpet.

Mike scurried after his ball. It rolled under an empty table near the front door, right behind the Rocket's table. As Mike picked up the ball, he heard a voice behind him. He glanced over to see the man in the fancy white suit talking to the Rocket.

"Winning the home run derby last night was really, really big. If you play well today, I *guarantee* you'll end up with a great contract for the next five years!" the man said. "Get as much playing time as you can. I'll do everything I can to help get you a huge contract!"

The Rocket nodded. "I'll do whatever it takes to get out on the field and show them what I can do," he said. "Tonight's the night!"

Mike backed away quietly and hurried to catch up to Kate. She was waiting for him in the hallway.

"I found out who the practical joker is!" Mike said.

Kate's eyes grew wide. "Who?"

"The Rocket!" Mike said. "I just heard him talking to that guy in the white suit. I think he's the Rocket's agent. The agent says if the Rocket gets more playing time, he'll get a better contract! The Rocket's trying to make himself look *good* and Josh look *bad*!"

A Slippery Situation

Andy was waiting for Kate and Mike near the entrance to the stadium. Behind him on the field, players were stretching and running sprints.

"Did you find out anything?" Andy asked. "I'll bet it was one of the National League players in the home run derby!"

"No," Kate said. "But you're close. It was one of the *American* League players in the home run derby."

"That doesn't make sense," Andy said.

"Why would someone want to hurt their own team?"

"Because they could get more playing time if one of the other players couldn't play," said Mike. "Like one of the two catchers."

Andy looked shocked. "You think the Rocket is the practical joker?" he asked.

"Mike overheard him talking to his agent at breakfast," Kate said. "He'll get more TV time if your father doesn't play. If the Rocket does well, he'll get a much bigger contract. He can make a lot of money if your father sits on the bench."

A shrill whistle brought everyone's attention to the dugout. Sparky called out for the team to gather. Mike, Kate, and Andy bounded down the aisle to the edge of the dugout.

Sparky paced back and forth. "I want everyone sharp for tonight's all-star game," he

said. He rapped his clipboard. "And no funny business! We have a game to win. Before we break, let's go over the notes."

Sparky glanced down at the clipboard. The paper was blank. He flipped it and examined the other side. It was blank as well. He reached up and scratched just behind his ear. "Darn it, now! Who took my notes? I just wrote them on the clipboard a few minutes ago."

Most of the players shook their heads. "Don't know, Coach," said one.

Finally, a player on the far side of the bench spoke up. "Did you write them with this?" he asked, holding up a black pen.

Sparky nodded.

"That's the problem," the player said. "My son has one of these." He took the pen and wrote *hello* on a scrap of paper and waited. There was silence in the dugout. A few players coughed and cleared their throats.

After another minute, Sparky dug his foot into the floor. "And your point is?" he asked.

The player looked at the piece of paper. "There," he said. The word had vanished!

"The old disappearing ink joke! Someone left a bunch of these pens around the dugout," the player said. "You must have picked one up and written your notes with it."

Sparky looked as if he were about to say something, but bit his lip. He tossed the clipboard on the bench instead. "That's it. Hit the fields, everyone. In an hour, we'll go over the lineup. I'm making some changes," he said, glaring at Josh.

The players filed out to the field. When Josh stood up, Sparky tapped him on the shoulder with the pen.

"If I find out that you're pulling any more practical jokes, the joke will be on you," Sparky warned him. "I'll bench you for the entire game!"

Josh held up his hands. "I didn't have anything to do with the pens," he said. "Honest! I'm not the one pulling practical jokes."

Sparky's eyes narrowed. He pushed his face up close to Josh's. "Well, someone is, and you're the biggest suspect. One more joke and it won't be the ink that's disappearing. It'll be you!"

Josh stared back at Sparky. Then he grabbed his glove and ran up the stairs to the field.

Without a word to his friends, Andy dashed after his dad to the bull pen. Kate gave Mike a shrug and followed Andy. When they reached him, he was standing on the warning track in front of the bull pen.

Josh had set up on one of the two pitching lanes. The Rocket was catching on the other one.

Andy put his head down and whispered to Kate and Mike, "We need to keep an eye on the Rocket. I'm going to make sure he doesn't do anything else to my dad!"

Two pitchers started their warm-up. *Swish! Thwap! Swish! Thwap!* The pitcher on the far lane threw one fastball after another into the Rocket's glove. Andy was so busy watching the Rocket, he didn't notice the problem his dad was having.

Kate nudged Mike. "Something's wrong with Josh," she whispered. She didn't want Andy to hear.

Swish! Zwack! Plop! Swish! Zwack! Plop!

Josh caught each pitch. But right after the ball zapped into his glove, it slipped out and plopped on the ground. It happened again and again!

Andy finally noticed. "Oh no," he moaned.

The Rocket called over to Josh, "Trying to make the ball disappear like Sparky's notes? Not sure that's a good idea! Or did you just have too much butter on your toast this morning?"

"Knock it off, Rocket," Josh called back. "Something funny is happening here."

"That's not what Sparky thinks," the Rocket said. He let out a little laugh. "Seems like you're in royal trouble with him! Get it? *Royal* trouble?"

Josh lifted up his catcher's mask. He dipped a finger into the palm of the glove. Then he smeared something on his pants.

"Someone put grease all over the inside of my glove!" Josh said loudly.

Benched!

"Andy, can you run back to my locker and get my other catcher's glove?" Josh called to his son. "You know where it is."

"Sure, Dad," Andy said, giving his dad a grin. He sprinted across the grass and disappeared into the dugout. A few minutes later, he came back with the glove.

Josh slipped it on and flexed it open. He pounded the palm a few times. "No grease in this one," he said. "Thanks!" He flipped his catcher's mask down and went back to practicing.

Andy ran over to Mike and Kate.

"I didn't like the way the Rocket taunted your father," Kate said. "He's definitely the prime suspect."

Andy nodded. "That's what I think," he said. "We need to keep our eyes on him."

At eleven-thirty, the bull pen phone rang. It was time to head back for a meeting. One by one, the players grabbed their gloves and hats and headed to the dugout. The Rocket and Josh took off their catcher's gear and jogged across the field.

Mike, Kate, and Andy sat in the empty seats right next to the dugout. They could see everything. Most of the players were just hanging out. Josh sat on the bench, cleaning off his glove. The Rocket stood near them, at the edge of the dugout. He kept reaching into a white plastic bucket, picking something up, and dropping it back into the bucket again.

"What's he doing?" Andy asked. "They usually keep bubble gum in there."

Mike perked up. "I'll go find out," he said. He leaned over the dugout railing as the Rocket played with the bucket of gum. Then the Rocket noticed Mike watching him.

"Can I have a piece?" Mike asked.

"Um, I guess so," the Rocket said. "You sure you want it?"

Mike gave him a big smile and nodded. "Yeah," he said. "Can I have some for my friends, too?"

The Rocket laughed. He looked at Kate and Andy. "Here you go!" he said. "That should fire you up!"

Mike took the gum back to Andy and Kate.

"It's just gum," Mike said. He tossed them both a piece and unwrapped one for himself.

Mike was just about to put it in his mouth when Kate's hand shot out and stopped him.

"I'm not sure that's a good idea," she said.

"Why not?" Mike asked. "It says right here, Pete's Picante Gum! Geez, Kate, you're always so suspicious. Looks like cinnamon to me."

Kate shrugged. "Don't say I didn't warn you."

Mike rolled his eyes. He popped the piece of gum into his mouth and chewed away. Within a few seconds, his face turned beet red.

Mike waved his hands and said, "HAAAA-HAAAA ARRRGH!"

He ran up the aisle to a trash can at the top of the walkway. Andy and Kate rushed up the stairs after him. Mike hunched over the trash can and spit the gum into it. By the time Andy and Kate reached him, Mike had his hands on his hips. He was taking deep breaths.

"You don't look so good," Kate said.

Mike's tongue hung out. Beads of sweat rolled down his forehead. He shook his head slowly. "Hot. Hot. Hot," he panted.

"What's the matter?" Andy asked. "You okay?"

Mike caught his breath. "I'm fine," he said. "But that gum isn't. The Rocket just gave me a handful of red-pepper gum!"

Kate took out her piece of gum and pointed to the red wrapper. "*Picante* means *spicy* in Spanish!" she told him. Kate was learning Spanish from her dad.

Mike sighed. "Why didn't I listen to you?"

Kate knuckled him on the head. "I wonder that all the time!"

Andy smiled. "Don't you see what this means?" he said. "The Rocket knew it was pepper gum! We should tell Sparky. It will prove the Rocket's the joker, not my father."

They rushed to the edge of the dugout, but Sparky had already started the team meeting. There was no way to interrupt. Mike, Kate, and Andy stood off to the side, listening. After ten minutes, Sparky stopped talking to take a drink. He picked up a large paper cup and filled it with red PowerPunch from a plastic jug at the end of the bench.

A few seconds later, one of the players snickered and pointed at the coach. A line of red PowerPunch dribbled down from a small hole in the bottom of the paper cup. It turned almost the entire front of Sparky's white uniform red!

Sparky finally noticed everyone laughing. "What's so funny?" he shot out.

The players instantly went quiet. Someone pointed to the front of his shirt.

Sparky looked down and saw the long red stain on his shirt. Without another word, he crumpled the paper cup and threw it into the trash can. Then he turned to face Josh.

"That's your final practical joke, Robinson!" he bellowed. "Don't practice any more, because you're benched!"

One of the outfielders jumped up. "Hey, Coach, you can't take Josh out! He's one of our best players," he pleaded. "We need him on the field tonight!"

"If we're going to beat the National League, we can't have jokers fooling around," Sparky snapped. "We need to focus on winning, not having fun! End of story. Everyone back out for more practice! Josh, stay here. If anything else happens, you won't even suit up for tonight's game!"

Concretes and Clubs

"Benched?" Andy wailed. "Benched? My dad doesn't have anything to do with the jokes! It's not fair! The all-star game is one of the biggest events of his life!"

The players jogged back onto the field. Some of them patted Josh on the shoulder as they went by. After a minute or so, Josh went into the locker room. The Rocket was the last to leave the dugout. On the way, he noticed Mike, Kate, and Andy standing near the infield fence. He nodded at Mike. Then he opened his mouth wide, panted with his tongue hanging out, and gave a big laugh!

Kate gripped the infield railing hard and stamped her foot. "That's so mean!" she said.

"Come on. Sparky is still in the dugout!" Andy said, opening the gate to the field. "We'll tell him what the Rocket did to Mike. Then he'll know who's playing the jokes!"

Sparky stood in the corner, writing on his clipboard. Andy tapped him on the arm. Sparky spun around.

"Oh, hello," Sparky said. "You're Josh's kid, right?"

Andy nodded. "Yes, I'm Andy. These are my friends Mike and Kate. We have something to tell you."

"What is it, son?" Sparky growled, looking at his watch. "I've got a team to run."

Mike stepped forward. He explained how

the Rocket handed out the spicy gum. He told Sparky what he'd overheard the Rocket and his agent talking about during breakfast, and how the Rocket had taunted Josh during practice.

"See?" Andy said. "The practical joker isn't my dad. It's the Rocket!"

Sparky listened patiently, but shook his head. "Sorry, Andy. I don't believe the Rocket is the joker. Everyone knows that your dad is famous for practical jokes. Of course, you'd love to have someone else to blame, son, but my decision stands. Josh is benched." Sparky snapped around and strode out to where the team was practicing near the right-field wall.

Mike, Kate, and Andy were speechless for a minute.

Then Andy kicked at the red dirt of the warning track. "Now what?" he asked.

Kate studied the stadium. "We need a break," she said. "And I'm hungry."

Mike rubbed his stomach. "Me too!" he said. "I have to get rid of the taste of that gum." He stuck out his tongue. "It still burns."

Kate grabbed Andy's arm and led him up the stairs. "Let's get something to eat," she said. "My mom gave me money."

A wide walkway ran around the edge of the Royals ballpark. Mike, Andy, and Kate headed for the food shops behind the giant scoreboard in center field. Suddenly, music blared over the stadium's speakers, followed by a loud splashing noise.

"The fountains!" Andy said. He pointed at the long black fountains that ringed the out-field walls. The music kicked up again, and water from the fountains sprayed high into the air. Blue, red, and yellow lights shone up

from the bottom of the fountains. Sheets of
water cascaded down the front of the black
fountain walls.

"They look cool during a game," Andy said. "Especially night games, when you can really see the colored lights!"

All around them, ballpark workers were getting ready for the all-star game. Vendors were loading up souvenir stands. Food-stand workers were stocking racks full of potato chips, caramel corn, and cotton candy.

Up ahead, a door to one of the shops opened. "Hey, Andy!" a man called. The door opened wider, and the man waved Andy over.

"That's Mr. Donovan," Andy said to Mike and Kate. "He owns Donovan's Custard. It's the best frozen custard in Kansas City. Maybe the best anywhere!"

"I'm just opening for the day and need some taste testers," Mr. Donovan said. "You kids up for it?"

"Sounds great!" said Mike. "But what's frozen custard?"

Mr. Donovan laughed. "You must not be from around here. Frozen custard is like ice cream, but it's made just a little differently. It has eggs in addition to cream, sugar, and flavorings. I think you'll like it!"

Inside the store, shiny black-and-white tiles covered the walls. A long counter held all kinds of toppings, from peanuts to gummy bears. Two large silver machines stood behind the counter.

"How about one of our famous concretes?" Mr. Donovan asked.

Mike made a face. "No way. You've got candy bars, chocolate chips, and sprinkles. Why would anyone want something you make a sidewalk with?"

Mr. Donovan smiled. "A concrete is a frozen

custard loaded with all that stuff! They're called concretes because they're packed thick with mix-ins!"

A few minutes later, Mike, Kate, and Andy sat on the stools in the front window of the shop. Mike dug into his dirt-and-worms chocolate concrete. Kate took big bites of her peanut-butter-pretzel concrete. And Andy worked on his cherry-berry-banana concrete.

"This is the best ever!" Mike said in between mouthfuls. "My mouth feels cooler already!" He stuck out his tongue again.

After finishing their treats, they said goodbye to Mr. Donovan. The frozen custard had definitely cheered Andy up. But when he saw the team practicing on the field, he sighed.

"Unless we can think of something soon," he said, "my dad doesn't have a chance of playing tonight."

Mike tossed Andy his baseball. "Don't worry," he said. "We'll figure it out."

Andy rolled Mike's baseball from hand to hand. Finally, he shrugged. "I hope so." Then he smiled. "Hey, you guys want to see something really cool?"

Andy led Mike and Kate past Donovan's Custard to the area behind the outfield shops. It looked as if they had stepped into an amusement park! In front of them was a giant merry-go-round with colorful animals and bright lights. Nearby were batting cages, a miniature baseball field, and even a playground.

"Wow!" Kate said.

On the side was an area filled with curvy brick paths and swaths of green Astroturf. "They've got a minigolf course here?" Mike asked.

"Yup. The Kansas City Royals wanted

fun things for kids to do," Andy said. "So they added this outdoor adventure area. The minigolf is my favorite. It only has five holes, but they're all baseball-related."

Andy grabbed three golf clubs and a brightly colored ball from a box nearby. "I'm taking blue, for the Royals," he said.

Mike grabbed a green ball. Kate thought for a moment, then picked a shiny red ball. Andy passed out the clubs. "Lowest score for five holes wins!"

"I'll go first!" Mike said as he ran to the first hole. A huge white baseball stood in the middle of the fairway. To score, Mike needed to hit his ball through the small tunnel at the bottom of the baseball and into the hole at the far end of the green. He dropped his ball and swung away.

PLUNK!

The golf ball bounced off the side of the giant baseball and wedged against the stones on the edge of the course. Now the only way to get the ball in the hole was over a hump on the side of the baseball.

Kate shook her head. "Mike, you need to line up your shot first!" she said.

Mike grimaced. "I didn't want you two to feel bad when you miss the shot," he said. "But watch. I'm going to get a hole in one next."

It took Mike three more putts before his ball made it into the hole. Andy made it through the tunnel on the first try. He finished in one more hit. Kate took three. She went first on the next hole. A big brown pitcher's mound stood between the tee and a home plate with a hole at the end.

Kate took her time and lined up her shot. *THUMP.* A solid hit sent her red ball up and over the pitcher's mound. *CLUNK!* The ball dropped neatly into the cup. Hole in one!

"Woo-hoo! I guess that's what you call sliding into home," she said.

Andy scored in only two putts. Mike went next. He hit his ball so hard that it flew over the pitcher's mound and off the course!

After two holes, Andy and Kate were tied at four strokes. Mike had seven.

For the next shot, they had to hit the ball

through a baseball bat fence. There were only narrow holes between the bats. As Andy got ready to putt, Kate nudged Mike.

"Good idea back there," she whispered. "If we let Andy win, it might cheer him up. I'll do it, too."

Mike raised his eyebrows. "Uh, yeah. Right. Letting Andy win," he said, nodding. "I'll make sure not to do too well. That was my plan all along."

"And you're just the guy to do it!" Kate said with a wink.

Andy finished in just two shots, while Kate and Mike took three. On the fourth hole, they all got two.

The last hole was set up like an outfield wall. Three bright white jerseys of retired Royals players were painted on the wall. The golf ball had to go over a jump and into a small hole in the wall. Otherwise, it fell into a trap.

Mike went first. He chopped at the ball. It flew off the jump and sailed into the wall. *TWAP!* Straight into the trap. Kate hit hers too softly. It dribbled off the end of the jump into the pit.

"Nice shot, cuz," Mike said. He held out his hand and fist-bumped Kate. "Good job lining it up!"

Kate shook her head. "Your turn, Andy," she said.

"Watch this," Andy said. He placed his blue ball on the pad. He studied the wall and then swung neatly. The ball raced off the end of the ramp, straight into the hole in the wall. Andy won!

"Not bad," Kate said. "I guess you're the master!"

"Great shot, Andy," Mike added. "Maybe *you* should be telling both of us how to line up shots!"

Andy smiled wide for a moment. But then the smile faded. He pointed at the painted jerseys on the wall. "Those remind me of my dad. What if he doesn't play tonight?" Andy scuffed the ground with his sneaker.

Kate studied the jerseys. "Andy! That's it!" she said. "I know what we have to do! We need to search the clubhouse for evidence."

Mike snapped his fingers. "You're right," he said. "I'll bet there are clues in the Rocket's locker!"

Andy brightened up. "Great idea!" he said.

Kate, Mike, and Andy ran past the food stands to the main walkway. The team was still down on the field. But instead of running sprints or doing exercises, the players were standing in a large group. They had all dropped their equipment.

"That doesn't look right," Mike said. "Why aren't they practicing? What are they doing?"

Kate gulped. She couldn't believe her eyes. "I—I don't know," she stammered. "But they're pointing right at us!"

Fountains of Foam!

"What did we do?" Andy asked, holding up his hands.

Mike, Kate, and Andy looked at each other from head to toe. Nothing seemed out of the ordinary.

"Wait a minute," Mike said. "Shh! Something *is* different. It's quieter here."

Kate and Andy listened. They heard the sounds of a highway in the background. But nothing else.

"The fountains!" Mike said. "Why don't we

hear the fountains in the outfield?"

Kate peeked over the outfield seats. "Guys, they're not pointing at us!" she said. "They're pointing at the fountains!"

Mike and Andy took a few steps forward. Kate was right. When they had walked by earlier, the fountains were shooting water far into the air. Water had cascaded down the black walls behind the outfield fences.

But now the fountains were filled with foam! Huge white bubbles floated off in the wind. Jets of water blew hundreds of bubbles across the outfield. Waves of small bubbles washed down the walls of the fountains. It looked like a gigantic bubble bath gone mad!

Andy grabbed his forehead. "Oh no!" he said. "Someone put bubble bath in the fountains! My father always joked about doing it, but now someone actually did!"

Down on the field, the managers shooed the players back to their workouts. Stadium workers rushed around, trying to shut the fountains off. Large, soapy bubbles floated by. Kate caught a bubble in the palm of her hand. She looked at it for a moment, then blew it away.

"Hey, now's the perfect time to check out the clubhouse!" Kate said, startling Mike and Andy. "Everyone's busy. Come on!"

They ran along the walkway and down the stairs to the infield. They stopped just outside the American League's dugout. In right field, the team was busy exercising again. Nobody would notice them. Just as they were about to enter the locker room, Andy stopped short.

"Wait! What if the Rocket comes in and catches us?" he asked. "Kate, how about you guard the door? Whistle if you see anyone coming."

Kate nodded. She crouched near the top of the steps, where she had a good view of the field.

Mike and Andy raced down the stairs into the clubhouse.

The Royals' clubhouse looked more like a hotel conference room than a locker room. A thick carpet with a big Kansas City Royals logo covered the floor. Laundry carts, tables, chairs, and workstations were spread around the center of the room. Big TVs and pictures of the players hung on the walls.

"This is such a cool clubhouse!" Mike exclaimed. He looked around at all the baseball equipment. Each player's locker was really an open cubby with shelves, hooks, and room for lots of stuff.

Andy led Mike to Josh's locker. It was about halfway down on the right side. An extra uniform hung from the bar inside. Cleats sat in a bin at the bottom. On the side of the locker were newspaper stories about Josh. Mike saw a picture of Andy and Josh playing baseball. Josh's glove rested on a shelf.

Mike lifted the big brown catcher's mitt. It felt much heavier and thicker than his glove at home. Josh had wiped off most of the grease earlier, but Mike and Andy could see traces of the clear, slippery gel near the stitching and under the leather straps. They checked it thoroughly. But they didn't see anything that would prove that the Rocket had greased it.

"Shoot!" Andy said.

"Okay, time for plan B, then," Mike said. "The Rocket's locker. Which one is it?"

Andy pointed across the room. "It's over there," he said. "See the sign above it that says *Richards*?"

Mike started across the room to the locker.

But as he passed the long conference table, he pulled out one of the rolling high-backed leather chairs and dropped down in it. "Watch this!" he said. With a shove, he pushed off from the table and sailed across the carpet.

"Wheeee!" Mike called out.

"Mike! Put it back," Andy said. "We don't have much time."

Mike spun the chair around. He used his feet to push himself to the middle of the room. Then he slid the chair against the conference table and joined Andy at the Rocket's locker.

It looked like all the other lockers, with extra equipment, clothing, and shoes. The Rocket had taped two newspaper stories about himself to the side.

They nosed around, but after a few minutes Andy shook his head. "I don't see any clues," he said.

All of a sudden, a loud whistle pierced the air. Before they could move, Kate burst into the locker room.

"The Rocket's coming!" she said. Her eyes were big. "I saw him and Sparky heading this way!"

Mike heard the click of shoes on the con-

crete stairs outside. He looked around wildly. Where could they hide? None of the lockers had doors that closed.

"This way," Mike hissed. The conference table had given him an idea. It was just like breakfast all over again!

Mike pulled a chair out and signaled for

Kate and Andy to crawl under the table. He followed and pulled the chair after him. With all the chairs around the table, they couldn't see much, but that meant they couldn't be seen, either. Through the chairs, Mike could just make out the bottom of each locker.

A few seconds later, a pair of legs walked up to Josh's locker.

"That must be the Rocket," Andy whispered to Kate and Mike. "What's he doing?"

A Surprise

From under the table, it was hard to tell what the Rocket was doing. Mike saw him place a plastic Royals souvenir bag on the ground by the table. He pulled something out of the bag and then rustled around in Josh's locker.

Andy bit his lip and scowled. He looked as if he were about to say something, but Mike put a finger to his lips. He pointed to the plastic bag. Kate's eyes got wide. She nodded and snaked one hand out between the chairs. She snagged the bag and pulled it toward her.

They peeked inside. It was filled with things for practical jokes! Stink bombs. Fake insects. More disappearing ink pens. The Rocket's bag was loaded with trouble.

Andy's face broke into a wide smile. He gave Kate a thumbs-up. But Mike waved his hand furiously. He tapped his head as if he had an idea. Then he mouthed the words "Watch me."

The Rocket was still moving things around in Josh's locker. Hidden by the chairs, Mike reached out to the Rocket's shoes. Before Kate could pull him back in, Mike had quietly tied the laces on the Rocket's shoes together!

As Mike slid back under the table, Kate gave him a questioning look.

But Mike just smiled. Then he turned and shoved one of the big black chairs as hard as he could. The chair flew across the room.

"Hey, who's there?" the Rocket called out as the chair rolled across the floor. Kate, Mike, and Andy watched the Rocket's feet as he turned.

POING! The laces on his shoes snapped tight.

"Whoa!" the Rocket cried.

In an instant, his knees buckled. *UMPH!* The Rocket toppled to the clubhouse carpet in a heap!

Mike jumped out from under the table. "Don't move, Rocket!" he shouted. "We've caught you red-handed!"

Kate and Andy popped out in time to see the Rocket twisting around to face them.

Andy gasped. "Oh no!"

"*Oh no* is right!" Kate added.

"Hey, you're not the Rocket!" Mike said. "You're his agent!"

"Of course I am," the man said. He retied his shoes, then stood up and dusted himself off. "I'm Tom Clark." He scowled at Mike, Kate, and Andy. "What are you kids doing here? This is private property! Don't you have school or something?"

Andy stepped forward. "Yes, it's my *dad's* private property," he said. "We were watching you. What were you doing poking around in his locker? And what did you put in there?"

Clark glanced back at the locker. He read the name ROBINSON over the top of it. "Oh, uh, um, your dad's locker?" he stammered. "I—I thought this was the Rocket's locker."

"It's my dad's locker, and you know it," Andy said.

"Well, I was just leaving, kid," the agent said.

Kate peeked into Josh's locker. "You pulled something out of the plastic bag and put it in Josh's locker. What was it?"

Before the agent could answer, they heard footsteps. It sounded like baseball cleats coming down the stairs. Everyone froze.

Sparky walked into the locker room.

He looked around, lifted his baseball cap, and scratched the top of his head. "Some kinda trouble going on? I heard voices down here. What're y'all doing?"

Mike, Andy, the agent, and Kate started talking at once.

Sparky held up his hands for quiet. "All right, all right. That's enough," he said. He pointed at Andy. "Okay, what's going on?"

Andy explained how they saw the agent hide something in Josh's locker. When he finished, Sparky checked the top shelf. He grabbed a big white plastic bottle.

SUDZI'S SUPER FOAM

"This guy's the joker!" Mike cried. "Not Josh. He brought a whole bagful of practical jokes. We hid the bag under there." Mike

scooted under the table. He grabbed the bag and plopped it down in front of Sparky.

"That's not *my* bag," the agent said. "I've never seen it before."

"Oh really?" asked Kate. "Have you seen this before?" She held up a half-full bag that read PETE'S PICANTE GUM—HOT TIMES FOR YOUR MOUTH! "Or this?" she said, pulling out a small bottle with ITCHING POWDER printed on the front.

Andy reached into the bag and found a tube of clear grease and a small saw. "He used this grease on my dad's glove!" Andy exclaimed. "And this saw on the chair at the home run derby!"

The agent sniffed. His steely black eyes looked down at Andy. "Maybe you should ask your father about those," he said. "Because that bag's not mine."

Andy looked up at Sparky. "We saw him

bring the bag in," he said. "He took something out of it and put it in my dad's locker!"

Sparky stared at the bottle of Sudzi's Super Foam in his hand. Then he looked at the agent. On the floor, Kate kept digging through the bag.

"Well, it seems like we need to find out who really owns this," Sparky said. He nudged the plastic bag with his shoe. "That would tell us a lot."

Andy's face dropped. "How are we going to do that?" he asked. "It's impossible!"

Kate stood up. She was holding the bag. "No, it's not," she said. "Look at what I found at the bottom of the bag." She pulled out a stack of papers. She handed them to Sparky. "It looks like Mr. Clark printed out his emails."

Sparky held the top email at arm's length and read: "From: Tom Clark. To: Director,

Sports TV Channel Five. I'm ace catcher Rocket Richards's manager. I have inside information that the Rocket, and *not* Josh Robinson, will be starting in the all-star game this week. Make sure to keep your cameras on the Rocket during the game!"

The agent slumped against the wall.

Kate pointed to the date on the email. "This was sent almost a week ago!" she said. "Mr. Clark has been planning this all along!"

Sparky handed the papers back to Kate. "Looks like we've just caught ourselves an all-star joker," he said. "Why don't you take a seat over there while I call my bull pen? I have a few people who might want to talk to you, Mr. Clark!"

The agent shuffled over to the table. Sparky turned to Andy, Kate, and Mike.

"You kids can hang out in the dugout

while we get this sorted. We've got a few hours before game time," Sparky said.

Mike, Kate, and Andy headed for the door. They were just about to climb the stairs when Sparky stopped them.

"Andy!" he called.

Andy turned around. "Yes?"

"Uh, one more thing," Sparky said. "Can you tell your dad that I have something to say to him?"

A Friendly Shake

Sparky reached into the bucket of gum on the dugout steps. He pulled out a piece wrapped in bright red paper.

"Rocket! Here's another for you!" Sparky called. "I think you should eat every one we find!" He tossed the piece of Pete's Picante Gum at the Rocket.

The Rocket sat on the bench next to Josh. He caught the gum. "Come on, Coach," he said. "I had no idea that my agent was playing all those practical jokes! I thought it was Josh!"

"Thanks, buddy," Josh said. "I'll remember that next time you need something."

"Sorry, Josh," the Rocket said. "I should have believed you. People said my agent was ruthless, but I never thought he'd do something to hurt other players. I guess he figured if you were benched, I'd get more playing time. Then I'd get a better contract."

The Rocket tried to offer the gum to Josh, but Josh held up his hands and backed away. The Rocket slipped it into his pocket instead.

"Well, why'd you give a piece to Mike, then?" Andy asked the Rocket.

"Someone had just tricked me by giving *me* one," the Rocket said. "But I warned him. I told him he'd have a *hot* time!"

Sparky reached into the bucket again. This time he came up with a square piece of bubble gum. He ripped the white paper off

and popped it into his mouth. "That's better," he said, blowing a small pink bubble. "I want my boys to be hot on the field, not hot in the dugout!"

Kate, Mike, and Andy were sitting at the far end of the bench. Just then, Kate's cell

phone rang. She pulled the phone out of her
pocket and looked at the caller ID.

"It's my mom," Kate said. She answered
the phone and talked to her mother for a minute. Then she slipped the phone back into
her pocket.

"She wanted to know why we weren't in our seats!" Kate said. "So I told her we found better seats. *In the dugout!*" Kate high-fived Mike and Andy.

Sparky saw them high-fiving. "Nice view, huh?" he said, nodding at the field. "You guys can stay here all game, as long as you don't cause any trouble."

"Don't worry," Kate said. "I'll keep an eye on Mike. He's the one you have to worry about!"

"I'll be too busy watching the game to cause trouble tonight," Mike said. "I knew the all-star game would be great, but I never thought I'd see it from the dugout!"

"I'm just happy that my dad's back in the game," Andy said. "That's the best part."

"Speaking of being in the game ..." Sparky studied his clipboard for a moment. He took out a pencil and made some changes. "Now that we know who the real all-star joker is, I'll be putting Josh in the game first. Rocket, I'll see when I can work you in."

The Rocket smiled. "It's fine," he said. "Josh is a great catcher and a good hitter. I'll be proud to follow him!"

Josh raised an eyebrow. "Really, you don't care?" he asked. "What about your contract?"

"I want to get the best contract I can," the Rocket said. "But I'm going to find a new agent for that. One who's not trouble. I'm making a fresh start."

"That's good to hear," Josh said.

"So no hard feelings, then?" the Rocket asked Josh.

Josh shook his head. "No, no hard feelings."

"Thanks," the Rocket said. He held out his hand for Josh to shake. "Put her there."

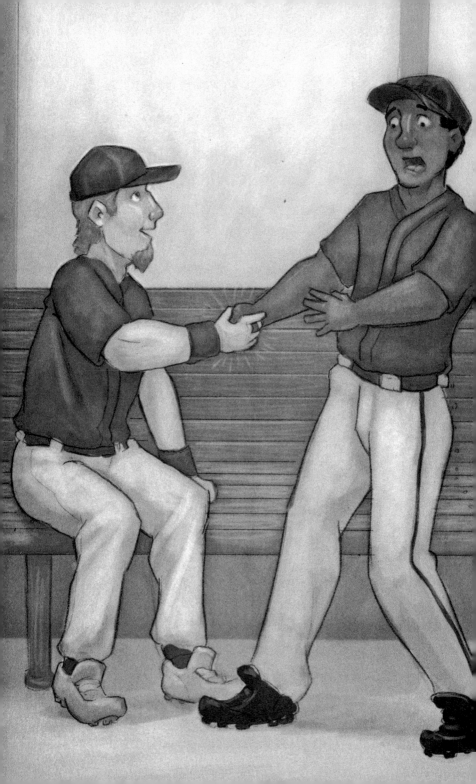

Josh smiled and reached out to grab the Rocket's hand.

BUZZZZ!

Josh yanked his hand away and jumped up off the bench.

"Hey! What was that?" Josh said, shaking his hand like crazy. "That felt like a swarm of bees!"

The Rocket opened his fist. Hidden in his palm was a small metallic joy buzzer.

"Gotcha!" the Rocket said. He winked and handed the buzzer to Josh. "But maybe from now on we should let you be in charge of the practical jokes!"

Dugout Notes
☆ Kauffman ☆ Stadium

Royals Hall of Fame. The Kansas City Royals have their own hall of fame! It's inside the stadium, behind the left-field wall. It has lots of great baseball artifacts, photos, and videos. It even has a supergiant baseball that's split open so you can see what's inside!

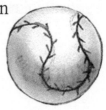

The Negro Leagues. Kansas City holds an important spot in baseball history. For many years, African Americans were not allowed to play major-league baseball. Instead, they played on teams in the Negro Leagues. One of the biggest, the Negro National League, was founded in Kansas City. The Negro Leagues ended after Jackie Robinson and other African American players started joining major-league teams.

Buck O'Neil. John Jordan "Buck" O'Neil was an important player and manager for the Kansas City Monarchs. The Monarchs were one of the most popular Negro League teams. O'Neil went on to become the first black manager in major-league baseball. He was also a scout for the Kansas City Royals. He loved to watch Royals games so much they gave him a special red seat behind home plate. Many people think he should be in the National Baseball Hall of Fame.

Barbecue. Kansas City is known around the world for its barbecue restaurants and food. Kansas City–style barbecue is meat that's slow-cooked over a smoky wood fire and covered with a thick, sweet sauce.

Fountains. Kauffman Stadium has the largest fountains and waterfalls in major-league baseball. The waterfalls are turned on during the game. The fountains spring up between innings. They also run before and after the game.

Scoreboard. The Royals' stadium has a *huge* scoreboard in center field. It's shaped like a home plate with a crown on top. The crown comes from the Royals' logo.

Prairie grass. Kansas City was near the starting point of many trails that led settlers to the American West in the 1800s. The settlers had to cross the Great Plains, which are filled with tall stalks of prairie grass. So the Royals planted lots of prairie grass around the outside of the stadium.

The Outfield Experience. Kauffman Stadium is really special because it has something called the Outfield Experience. It is a large patio behind the outfield filled with fun stuff for kids! There's a playground with tubes and slides, a baseball-themed merry-go-round, and even a short

minigolf course. It also has batting cages
for practicing your
swing, a base-
path run to test
your speed, and
a pitching mound
to clock your throws.

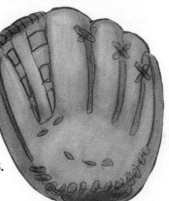

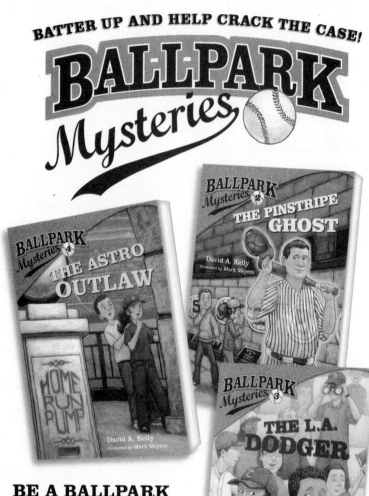